To Noah and Charlie
MT-H

To my husband, Andrew
YI

First edition 2022

Library of Congress Catalog Card Number pending
ISBN 978-1-5362-0430-8

21 22 23 24 25 26 APS 10 9 8 7 6 5 4 3 2 1

Printed in Humen, Dongguan, China

This book was typeset in Bauer Grotesk.
The illustrations were done in gouache and watercolor.

Candlewick Press
99 Dover Street
Somerville, Massachusetts 02144

www.candlewick.com

LOVE IN THE LIBRARY

Maggie Tokuda-Hall

illustrated by Yas Imamura

CANDLEWICK PRESS

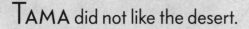

TAMA did not like the desert.

She brushed the dust from her eyes as she walked to the library.
The barbed wire fences and guard towers cast long shadows over her path.

She always did her best not to look at the guards.

Tama had taken the job in the library because she liked books. She didn't know how to be a librarian, but that didn't matter. In the camps, people did the jobs that needed doing, and that was that.

"Good morning, Tama," a voice boomed. It was George. Like every other day, George was waiting at the door for Tama with the stack of books he'd checked out only the day before.

"Good morning, George," Tama replied.

He waited for her to unlock the library, and then he followed her inside.

Tama and George had been in Minidoka for a year already.
She should have graduated college the previous summer,
but instead, Tama was here. All the Japanese Americans
from the West Coast were in prison camps like Minidoka.
Elderly people, children, babies.

It didn't matter who you were, just what you were—and being
Japanese American then was treated like a crime.

And though each camp was different, they were all the same.
Uncomfortable and unjust.

In the summer, it was brutally hot. In the winter, it was brutally cold. Rain in the fall and spring left mud around the latrines they all needed to use.

Whole families shared single rooms. No one had any privacy.

Tama did not know when she would leave Minidoka—if she ever would. But there was nothing to be done about that. So she worked in the library and watched as each day passed her by.

Some days, many people would come to the library and borrow something to read.

Other days, especially when it snowed, hardly anyone would brave the cold just for a book.

But most days were the same. Tama kept her eyes down and tried not to think about the life she used to have.

There was a word that described this, Tama knew: constant.

Constant questions. Constant worries. Constant fear.

But then, there was also George.
George and his big smile were constant.

And the books were constant company.
Which was nice. Tama loved books.
Caught in their pages were worlds bursting with
color and light, love and fairness.

Pressed between their covers were words that planted seeds in the garden of Tama's mind. How magical that—even in Minidoka—such a small little library could fit so much inside of its four walls!

Tama kept a word for that, too, nestled close to her heart.
"Miraculous," she whispered.

"What was that?" asked George.
His voice was so big it barely fit in the library. Tama blushed. Then she held up her finger to remind him of the rules. They were in a library, after all. George just went on grinning at her.

Tama wanted to smile back. She tried to focus on the things that made her smile—the boys outside, hollering and cheering as they played baseball. The books themselves and the smell of their pages.

But she could not make herself smile. She sighed.

"What's wrong?" George asked.

"Nothing. Or everything," Tama said. She did not need to tell him what she meant. He knew. Everyone in Minidoka knew. "I try not to complain. I know this isn't fair, but I also know there is nothing to be done. I try not to be afraid. But I'm just so—so—"

But she could not think of a word that was right. She was scared and sad and confused and frustrated and lonely and hopeful.

Maybe there was no word that fit. Maybe, for the first time in her life, there was no single word she could hold in her heart to help her understand. And that thought was so sad to Tama, so upsetting, that she felt the hot prickle of tears behind her eyes.

"Hey," George said. And for once, his voice was small
and soft. "There's a word for that, you know."

"There is?" Hope bubbled big and bold in Tama's heart.

"Human," George said.

He smiled his big smile, and Tama smiled back. She wiped her eyes. She held the word close to her heart and felt less alone than she had only a moment before.

"You can't possibly be reading all those books you check out," she said.

"No," he replied. "Do you see how long they are? I'm only human, you know."

"So then, why come every day?" She laughed. But George was not laughing.

And then for the first time she saw him, really saw George, and saw what he held close to his heart.

It was her.
Tama.

They were married, Tama and George, and their first son was born in Minidoka.
They hoped for the best.

Their love for the family they made was constant, even if the injustice their
family was created within was constant, too.

To fall in love is already a gift. But to fall in love in a place like Minidoka, a place built to make people feel like they weren't human—that was miraculous.

That was humans doing what humans do best.

"The miracle is in us," Tama wrote in her journal.
"As long as we believe in change, in beauty, in hope."

That miracle is hard to find sometimes. But it is in all of us.

AUTHOR'S NOTE

This is a true story. Mostly.

George and Tama are my maternal grandparents. They had five children, including my mother. They truly did meet in Minidoka, a Japanese incarceration camp in Idaho. Tama was the camp librarian. Their first son, Floyd, was born there. But the dialogue is imagined, save for one line:

"The miracle is in all of us." Those are Tama's exact words, taken from her journal.

After the nation of Japan attacked Pearl Harbor in 1941, Franklin D. Roosevelt signed Executive Order 9066, which caused citizens of Japanese ancestry on the West Coast to be "relocated." This was tidy language used to obfuscate the truth: that American citizens were to be wrongfully imprisoned for the crime of being Japanese.

The 120,000 Japanese Americans who were incarcerated lost their jobs, their homes, their educations, and their possessions. They had to go on short notice to relocation centers and then incarceration camps with only what they could carry. Family heirlooms, cherished belongings, pets—so much was left behind by necessity. They might need food, tools, clothes. They didn't know. They weren't told. And so they left their lives behind.

Robbed of their rights and their dignity, the Americans who found themselves in squalor and destitution made the best of their lives that they could in the camps. And that to me is the great wonder of this story. That even under those circumstances, that terrible injustice, Tama and George found love.

This is not to say that it was "worth it." Their improbable joy does not excuse virulent racism, nor does it minimize the pain, the trauma, and the deaths that resulted from it. But it is to situate it into the deeply American tradition of racism.

As much as I would hope this would be a story of a distant past, it is not. It's very much the story of America here and now. The racism that put my grandparents into Minidoka is the same hate that keeps children in cages on our border. It's the myth of white supremacy that brought slavery to our past and allows the police to murder Black people in our present. It's the same fear that brings Muslim bans. It's the same contempt that creates voter suppression, medical apartheid, and food deserts. The same cruelty that carved reservations out of stolen, sovereign land, that paved the Trail of Tears. Hate is not a virus; it is an American tradition.

And yet. And yet so many of us find improbable joy. Our capacious hearts find the love that our nation has denied us. Just as Tama and George did. In the face of all that hate.

Though it is always easier to destroy than it is to build, reminding myself of stories like Tama and George's reminds me to hope. To let my heart seek out the beauty and the peace the marginalized miraculously create for themselves. To let myself imagine a future where that love is not improbable, but easy. To force myself to fight for that future.

Because if we can fall in love, if we can find our joy, if we can find that miracle despite all of these truths—

What else can we do?

Tama and George Tokuda